Anna Sewell's
The Adventures of Black Beauty

Black Beauty Finds a Home

Adapted by I. M. Richardson
Illustrated by Karen Milone

Troll Associates

Library of Congress Cataloging in Publication Data

Richardson, I. M.
    Black Beauty finds a home.

    (Anna Sewell's The adventures of Black Beauty;
bk. 4)
    Summary: Black Beauty relates his experiences
with a cruel owner followed by his sale to three
ladies and his subsequent reunion with his stable
boy of ten years earlier.
    1. Horses—Juvenile fiction. [1. Horses—Fiction]
I. Milone, Karen, ill. II. Sewell, Anna, 1820-
1878. Black Beauty. III. Title. IV. Series:
Richardson, I. M. Anna Sewell's The adventures of
Black Beauty; bk. 4.
PZ10.3.R413An bk. 4   [Fic]   82-7024
ISBN 0-89375-816-7   AACR2
ISBN 0-89375-817-5 (pbk.)

I had been a fancy coach horse, and a fine riding horse. I had pulled rented carriages, and even a London cab. But I was no longer young, and now I was only a cart horse. The work was hard, but it was fair—at least at first. If my owner had been there all the time, my cart would never have been overloaded.

3

My owner, however, put a foreman in charge of loading my cart. When it was full, the foreman always had something else put on. "There's no sense in making two trips if one will do the job," he said. My driver often said that the extra weight was too much for me. But the foreman always had his way.

The worst part about being a cart horse was having to wear bearing reins. Bearing reins make a horse keep his head up high. Such reins make a horse look very fashionable, but they also make pulling a cart much harder. One day, I was trying to pull a very heavy load up a hill. I used all my strength, but could not get up very far. My driver grew angry and began to whip me.

Soon a lady called out, "Please stop whipping that poor horse! I'm sure he's doing the best he can." But the driver growled, "It's not good enough." Then the lady said, "But he can't use all his power. Please take those bearing reins off, and then see what your horse can do for you." My driver smiled and said, "Anything to please a lady." Then he removed the bearing reins.

How good it felt to stretch my neck again! The lady said, "Now speak kindly to him, and see what he can do." I put my head down, and threw my whole weight into pulling the heavy load. Slowly, but steadily, I made it to the top of the hill. After that, my driver stopped using the bearing reins—at least when we came to a hill.

The heavy loads continued, day after day. At the end of each day, I was put into an uncomfortable stall in a poorly lighted stable. The darkness did nothing to lift my spirits. Each morning, when I was led outside, the bright sunlight hurt my eyes. Several times, I stumbled as I left the stable, for I could hardly see where I was going.

I would have lost my sight if I had stayed there very long. But I was sold again before that happened. My new owner was Nicholas Skinner, and he was the meanest man I ever met. He owned a cab company, and he made his drivers and horses work very hard, seven days a week.

My life was now so miserable that I wished I could die and be out of my misery. One day, my wish nearly came true. I had been working since eight o'clock, and had already done a good day's work. We had just taken a man to the railroad station. My driver pulled up in line behind some other cabs that were waiting for a return fare.

Soon a family with a great deal of luggage came over to our cab.
The lady and the young boy got right into the cab. As the man
fussed over the luggage, the girl walked up and looked at me.
She said to the driver, "I think this horse is too weak to take all
of us." But the driver said, "Oh, don't you worry about that.
He's strong enough to get the job done."

Meanwhile, the porter had dragged another heavy trunk over to
the cab. He suggested that the gentleman ought to take two
cabs, because there was so much luggage. The gentleman came
around to the front of the cab and asked, "Can your horse pull
this by himself, or can't he?" The driver replied, "Oh, he can do
it all right, sir."

Then the girl began to plead with her father. "Please, Father," she cried. "This is too much for one horse." "Nonsense, child," he said. "The man must know his own business. Now get into the cab." Then box after box was put on top of the cab. When the heavy trunk was added, I could feel the springs go down.

Finally, everything was loaded, and the last of the boxes was tied down. The gentleman joined his family in the cab. The driver gave his usual jerk on the reins and snapped his whip, and we started out of the station. I had not eaten or rested all day, but I did my best to pull the heavy load.

When we came to Ludgate Hill, the load was too much for me.
The driver lashed me with his whip, but I could not keep the cab
moving. As I strained against my harness, my feet suddenly
slipped from under me! I fell to the ground with such force
that I could not catch my breath. I lay there and did not move.
I felt sure I was going to die.

I don't know how long I lay there, but finally I felt life coming back to me. I heard a gentle voice coaxing me to rise. Somehow, I staggered to my feet. The overloaded cab was gone. A kind stranger led me to a nearby stable, where I was fed and allowed to rest. Later, I was taken to Nicholas Skinner's stables.

In the morning, Skinner brought a doctor to see me. "This horse has been so overworked that he has no strength left," said the doctor. "Still, with six months of rest, he may be able to work again." Skinner growled, "I'm not running a rest home for tired horses. If he can't work, then he'll be sold to the butchers!"

"That would be a shame," said the doctor. It was his opinion that Mr. Skinner should feed me well and give me plenty of rest for the next ten days. "By then, he will be well enough to bring a decent price at the horse sale outside London," explained the doctor. Skinner agreed. With each passing day, I began to feel better, as I gained a little of my strength back.

At the horse sale, I was put with several other horses who were either lame, old, or broken-down. Some of the men who came to this part of the horse sale were very poor. Some were tough men who would be very hard on any horse they owned. But a few were kind and gentle, and I would not have minded much if one of them had bought me.

Presently, an old gentleman farmer and a young boy began looking me over. "He must be thirteen or fourteen years old," said the gentleman, after he had looked at my teeth. The boy said, "Let's buy him, Grandfather. You could make him young again, like you did with Ladybird." The gentleman laughed, and said, "I can't make all old horses young, you know!"

20

Then the man who was selling me for Mr. Skinner spoke up. "The horse doctor said that six months of rest in a good pasture would make him as good as new," he said. The old gentleman looked me over again, and said, "What is the lowest price you will accept?" Before long, a servant was taking me home to my new master's farm in the country.

I was turned out into a large meadow that had a shed in one corner. Every morning and night, I received hay and oats. The boy came down to see me every day. His name was Willie. Sometimes, he brought me a piece of carrot or a slice of apple. Sometimes he just stood by me and talked to me while I ate my oats.

Sometimes Willie brought his grandfather down to see me. The old gentleman always looked carefully at my legs. One day, he said, "He's coming along well. I think we shall see some real progress in the spring." Over the winter, my legs grew much stronger. And by March, I felt younger than I had felt in years.

The old gentleman had me hitched up to a light four-wheeled carriage, and he and Willie took me out for a drive. My legs no longer had any trace of stiffness, and I pulled the carriage with perfect ease. "By summer, he will be as good as Ladybird," said the man. "We must start looking for a quiet home for him —a nice place where he will be well cared for."

One summer day, the groom took an unusually long time brushing me. I sensed that something special was going to happen. When he hitched me up to the carriage, I saw that there was even extra polish on my harness! As Willie and his grandfather climbed into the carriage, they seemed happy and a little anxious at the same time.

We started off down the road. Before long, we came to a nice house with a pretty lawn. We went up the drive and stopped at the door. Willie got out and rang the bell. He asked if Miss Ellen was at home, and was told that she was. Then Willie's grandfather got out of the carriage and went into the house. Willie stayed outside with me.

Ten minutes later, the gentleman returned, followed by three ladies. They all came and looked at me. The youngest of the ladies—Miss Ellen was her name—said she liked me. But the eldest one was not so sure. The third lady said that they would try me for a few days. If I did not work out, then I would be returned.

The next morning, the ladies' coachman came to get me. At first he was pleased. But then he saw the scars on my knees, and said, "This horse has fallen, sir. I am surprised that you would recommend him so highly." Willie's grandfather said, "If he has fallen, I am sure it was not his fault. If he is not as safe as any horse you ever drove, you may send him back."

So the coachman brought me home with him. As he was grooming me, he noticed a special mark I had. He exclaimed, "Why, I once cared for a horse that had this very mark. Could it be? Are you really Black Beauty?" Of course, I could not tell him that I was. But he knew. He was Joe Green, who had been my stable boy at Squire Gordon's, nearly ten years ago.

That afternoon, I was hitched up to a small, two-wheeled carriage, and brought to the ladies' front door. Miss Ellen was going to try me, and Joe Green would go along. I found that the lady was a good driver. She seemed pleased with me. Joe told her that he was sure I was Squire Gordon's old Black Beauty.

When we returned to the house, Miss Ellen praised me, and she told the other ladies what Joe had said. "I must write to Mrs. Gordon at once," she added. "How pleased she will be to learn that her favorite horse has come to us." Within a week, it was decided that they would keep me, and that they would call me by my old name of Black Beauty.

My work is easy here, and my spirits are high. Joe Green is the best and gentlest of grooms, and Willie comes to visit me whenever he can. But best of all, my mistresses have promised that I shall never be sold. And sometimes, when I am not quite awake, I even fancy I am a young colt again—running beneath the apple trees in the meadow where I was born.